This igloo book belongs to:

....

igloobooks

Published in 2022
First published in the UK by Igloo Books Ltd
An imprint of Igloo Books Ltd
Cottage Farm, NN6 0BJ, UK
Owned by Bonnier Books
Sveavägen 56, Stockholm, Sweden
www.igloobooks.com

0522 003
4 6 8 10 9 7 5 3
ISBN 978-1-80022-576-3

Written by Stephanie Moss
Illustrated by Heather Burns

Designed by Justine Ablett
Edited by Stephanie Moss

Printed and manufactured in China

CURLY KITTY

igloobooks

Curly's **FLUFFY** ringlet fur is stylish and unique.

But sometimes, things get tangled up and stuck there for a week!

Because this **curly** kitten
has such **twirly**, frizzy hair...

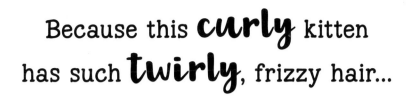

... SHE REALLY DOESN'T FEEL THAT SHE FITS IN ANYWHERE.

So, she creeps out of her basket
where her sleek-furred family sleeps...

... until she finds a field
full of curly-coated sheep!

She asks them, "Can I play with you?" The sheep all nod and bleat.
But soon, she's tired of chewing grass. There's nothing else to eat!

She spots a group
of llamas and she
sneaks among the herd.

At last, she fits right in
because they're all so

FUZZY FURRED!

"Help us carry these," they say.
"We all wear heavy packs."

But Curly needs to rest.
She cries out,

Ow, my
aching back!

"Will I ever find someone," she asks,
"who's just like me?"

And then, a glimpse, a glance,
of **FRIZZY** ringlets. Could it be?

She follows her new **FLUFFY** friend, and then, to her surprise...

... a curly monster
leaps
right out.

Ahhh,
help me!

Curly cries.

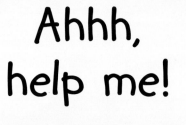

She runs till she can run no more. She's almost given up.
But Curly stops and stares when she sees one big, hairy pup!

Hello,

Curly says to him.

Hello,

he says to her.

They look into each other's eyes, and Curly starts to purr.

His **FLUFFY** fur has ringlets and his twirly coat is long.
Is being with this **FRIZZY** dog where Curly should belong?

They love to play together. Yes, it seems a perfect fit...

until her friend says something that she doesn't like one bit.

"It's time to get our hair cut."
As he says it, her jaw drops.
He shows her to the salon,
where her curls will get the chop.

PURR-FECT * POOCHES

"Sometimes, I'm the odd one out," says Curly. "Yes, that's true.
But I still want to look like me, and you to look like you."

So, Curly says goodbye, and
then she cries some little tears.
She blinks them all away...

... and then a **HAPPY** sight appears.

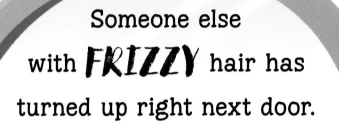

Someone else with **FRIZZY** hair has turned up right next door.

She **TIPTOES** in behind him...

... and she **_creeps_** across the floor.

It's another salon! She hears SNIPPING everywhere. She runs, till someone yells out...

I wish I had curly hair!

Standing there is someone who has hair so smooth and sleek,
this time, tears of happiness roll down our Curly's cheeks.

She ties her fur with **ribbons...**

... and she gives her **pretty bows.**

Because, hair straight or curly, friends make sure that their **LOVE** shows.

Curly thought a **FLUFFY** friend would help her to belong.
And then, she would fit in...

Of course,
she has done all along.